More praise for *Becon...*

"From the brilliant and prolific pen of Paul Beckman comes the compelling, funny, heartbreaking novella-in-flash, *Becoming Mirsky*. This collection of short stories follows the life of Reuven Mirsky from his Jewish boyhood in the projects of the Bridgeport. CT, to his service in the Air Force, and on to a new life in New Haven Connecticut suburbs. This is a layered story of place and family, of tradition and loss and survival. The child of a broken home, Mirsky is perennially misunderstood and emotionally neglected. Yet he faces the world with resilience, rebelliousness, and a sarcastic tongue that gets him into no end of trouble. The writing all through is deft and beautifully distilled. In these pages, Beckman has given us an unforgettable story of disarming courage and wit and sensitivity."
—Kathy Fish, author of *Wild Life: Collected Works*

"In Paul Beckman's unmistakable voice, a comfortable cup of coffee with a stiff shot of scotch, we meet (or better, examine) his recurring character, Reuven Mirsky, with all of the kid-of-the-fifties memories, so vividly drawn—lemon ices and paper routes—and the characters that inhabit Mirsky's world, a Bar-Mitzvah ruining Rabbi, Mirsky's kosher soap mother, and the father who only made guest appearances from time to time. A poignant, heart-tugging, witty, and ultimately triumphant story. A wonderful and memorable read."
—Francine Witte, author of *Just Outside the Tunnel of Love*

"When master flash fiction writer Paul Beckman put pen to paper for *Becoming Mirsky*, he demonstrated why he's been selected for a Norton Anthology, a winner for Best Small Fictions, and a winner of Fiction Southeast's prize. *Becoming Mirsky* is as good as it gets, following the life of Mirsky, a Jewish boy growing up in poverty in the projects of Bridgeport, Connecticut, and experiencing a rough, yet incredibly realistic, life, even among his closest family members. Becoming Mirsky illustrates how we rise above, move on, and become more."
—Niles Reddick, author of *Drifting too far from the Shore, Reading the Coffee Grounds, & Road Kill and Other Oddities*

"Beckman hits it out of the park, again. In *Becoming Mirsky*, a sidesplitting flash fiction bildungsroman that traces the trials of a young man growing up in Marina Village, a public housing project, Beckman sketches with his signature hilarity and warmth, the fraught path to adulthood for Mirsky. Sometimes innocently, and sometimes not-so-naively, Mirsky navigates his way among hardscrabble family, neighbors, and schoolmates. In adventures that range from delivering groceries past a dead man's body in a funeral parlor, to relishing the thought of one day becoming a successful shoe salesman so that he can smell the tantalizing scent of new shoe leather, Mirsky gradually learns the ways of the world. And as he recounts his hilarious adventures, readers learn that Mirsky's world, while uniquely colorful, if at times hardboiled, is not so terribly different from their own."

—**Brad Rose, author of *Lucky Animals* and *No. Wait. I Can Explain***

BOOKS BY PAUL BECKMAN

Flash Fiction

Novella

Becoming Mirsky

Paul Beckman

Červená Barva Press
Somerville, Massachusetts

Červená Barva Press
P.O. Box 440357
W. Somerville, MA 02144-3222

www.cervenabarvapress.com

Bookstore: www.thelostbookshelf.com

Cover photo: "Silhouette of Man Wearing Hat During Night Time" Courtesy Pexels: Cottonbro Studios

Cover design: Karen Schauber

ISBN: 978-1-950063-78-9

Library of Congress Control Number: 2023946777

ACKNOWLEDGMENTS

My thanks to the publishers of the following magazines who have published the following stories in the current or modified form and in the same or changed title:

Bartleby Snopes, Flash Fiction Magazine, The Wagon Magazine, We Are a Website, Journal of Microliterature (2), This Zine will change your life, Anti-Heroin Chic, Literally Stories, Unbroken Journal, Fiction on the Web, Eunoia Review, Spelk, New Vilna Review, Short Story Library, Story Bytes, Flash Frontier, The Airgonaut, (b)OINK, Matter Press, Flash Boulevard, Short Story Library, Strands International, Free Flash Fiction, Yellow Mama

I would like to thank the following people for their advice, encouragement, and most of all, their love of Mirsky.

Nancy Stohlman, Robert Scotellaro, Kathy Fish, Karen Schauber, Francine Witte, The FBombers staff & audience @ KGB, The Fbomb Zoomers, Joshua Beckman, and of course Gloria Mindock.

TABLE OF CONTENTS

Becoming Mirsky

What For

My mother had to switch the baby from her right arm to her left so she could reach around my brother to stop me from laughing with a good twisting pinch on my arm and that changed my laughter to crying which made her even madder telling me that people were watching us create a scene and she said, "stop crying this instant or you'll get what for when we get home." And all the time she was talking her lips were pursed and my mother, staring straight ahead, turned into the family ventriloquist and I was the dummy. I didn't want to get 'what for' when I got home so I took big gulps of air to try and stop my crying and my mother reached across in front of my brother and pinched my leg saying, 'I told you to stop" and I couldn't and she told me "Wait till I get you home and I'll give you something to cry about." And I never understood why laughing was bad and crying was better and I didn't even try to stop crying and people on the bus turned to see what was going on and that infuriated my mother even more and I saw her snake her arm behind my brother heading towards my four-year old self and I didn't want another pinching and another 'what for' so when the bus stopped I ran out the door not caring where I was or where I was going and I later realized I was going to get "it" again for not looking both ways before crossing the street which I wasn't supposed to do without holding a hand and the tears in my eyes kept me from seeing the car even though I swore later that I looked both ways and looking up at my mother from my hospital bed she said, "Liar" without moving her lips.

Day One

We moved to Marina Village, the projects, six years ago today. There is no marina, and it is certainly not a village but a bunch of two-story brick buildings with six apartments in each. Mom was miserable and trying not to let us see her crying. But we kids were thrilled—a 3-bedroom apartment with a kitchen, dining area, and a living room that smelled of new paint and cleaning fluid. We also had a tiny fenced-in dirt back yard and we were only a half-block from the corner store with its pinball machine, and a half block the other way to the bus stop.

Aunt Lizzy was there to help Mom and a few of the uncles came in a borrowed pickup truck. They moved what furniture we had or was given to us. On the way, we passed a few people sitting on their curbs surrounded by furniture waiting for their movers or families to help them load and move to their new houses. The furniture was in piles, not neatly stacked.

"They were all evicted," Uncle Carl said. "Oh," I replied before I got home, and Mom told me what it meant. "That's our next stop," she said bitterly.

By mid-afternoon, we were moved in and moving things around. At 5 pm mom was starting to cook dinner when the first knock on the door came, and I ran over hoping for a new friend who wanted to play ball.

Holding out an empty coffee cup the boy asked, "My Mum wants to know if she can borrow a cup of sugar. She'll return it on payday."

"I'm sorry," Mom said. "We haven't had a chance to go shopping yet."

"Momma Momma, I saw a big bag of sugar in the food closet."

"Yes, you did. It's a sugar bag that's empty of sugar and only has flour in it."

I knew Momma was wrong, but I also knew better than to correct her in front of others.

After Momma closed the door, she went into the living room and called her sister, Lizzy. I sat on the top of the stairs and listened. "It's started. The rich Jews move in so let's get some free stuff before someone else gets to them first."

Shabbos Goy

Shabbos Goy— A gentile doing physical work for a Jew on the Sabbath.

This Rabbi of my youth who shall be nameless because I swore to myself that I would never utter his name again, called me into his office one Saturday morning. In this Orthodox Shul, only those saying Kaddish stood or even remained in the Shul. The Rabbi would leave the bema during this prayer. His parents were still living, and he used this time to take a break from leading the services.
This is when he called me in.
His office was very small and windowless, and the walls showed leak marks. His smell was the smell of the room, and I felt a little nauseous as I always did when I had to be in his office. The floor was littered with books and papers, and there was room left only for the two wooden slatted folding chairs that faced his desk.
"Sit down," the Rabbi said. I'd been there many times before, too many, and not once had he asked me to sit. Knees knocking, I sat.
"Rueven, I want you to go to my house and do something for my wife." He took off his glasses, fogged them with his breath, and wiped them with his tie. He had never called me by my first name before. I always believed that he thought I only had one name—Mirsky.
"Yes, Rabbi. What would you like me to do?"
"I want you to light the gas stove for her." I noticed his frayed white shirt as he took off his tallis and hung it up. He sat down. His collar was dirty, too. I saw the Rabbi had a bunch of long black hairs growing out of his ears.
"It's Shabbos, Rabbi. What about Mr. Farley?" I asked.
Mr. Farley owned the small variety store across the street from our Shul. He was the person who would always turn on or off the lights on Shabbos. He was our Shabbos Goy, and was relied on heavily. In fact, if he didn't unlock the door, no

one else would. Turning on lights, locking doors, any manual labor was not permitted, so we relied on Mr. Farley.

"Mr. Farley is ill today," the Rabbi said with a hint of exasperation in his voice. "The first time in over twenty-five years he can't do his duties. And to think, just last month the congregation presented him with a special "Shabbos Goy Plaque" at a Sunday Men's Club Brunch. But today, even from his sickbed, he came and opened the Shul, turned on the lights, and only then went home. I would have had him do it, but he can't, and my wife, who, as you and everyone else knows, is a little scatterbrained, forgot to light the stove before sundown yesterday. So, I need someone to do this and I'm sending you."

"Why can't it wait until sundown today, Rabbi?"

Rising from his chair and leaning over his desk glaring at me, he said, "Don't question me. Go to my house."

"But it's a sin, Rabbi. I don't want to sin." I stood in my hand-me-down blue serge suit, hands in coat pockets, shuffling my feet, looking down at my shoes.

"Who are you to tell a Rabbi what is and what isn't a sin, you little pisher? If I tell you it's okay to do something then it's not a sin. Understand?"

"No."

"Go now, Mirsky," he yelled. "Do you need more trouble than you already have in this world?"

I was looking down at my scuffed shoes, realizing I was getting into trouble, and turned red. Not moving, I said, "Why doesn't your wife light the oven, Rabbi?"

"Shame on you for questioning me and mentioning my wife."

"But . . ."

"If you don't do this, Mirsky, I'll tell your mother that you don't know your Hebrew well enough to have a Saturday Bar Mitzvah. Remember, you don't pay dues here. You're a charity case." The Rabbi looked satisfied with himself. "You'll do your Haftorah on a Monday when all of your friends are in school. Do we understand each other?"

He had me do other things in the past because we were poor and couldn't afford the dues. "It's your way of repaying the Shul. You just can't take, take, take. You must do some giving," he said, more than once.

My mother, like every other woman in the congregation, loved the Rabbi. But with the Rebbetzin, it was a different story. She and the Rabbi never walked together, she always walked or stood behind him and I often heard him call her a klutz and make fun of her to others while she stood there. When she lost the last baby, she didn't come to Shul for a month. The Rabbi said she felt ashamed for stumbling down the basement stairs and having to stay in the hospital for almost a week. He told his congregants that she had miscarried and to please let her be and not visit her. This made the women love him more and gossip about his wife being a burden to such a fine young man. It was not unusual for him to be invited for dinner at a congregant's house and not bring his wife along.

So, I cleaned the benches, waxed the Ark, picked up papers around the Shul, and did what no one else wanted to do. But this was different. I didn't understand why the Rabbi's wife wasn't in Shul and sitting in the balcony with the other women, and why she needed the oven turned on during Shabbos.

The Rabbi got up, put on his tallis, and returned to the bema. I slowly walked to the Rabbi's house kicking stones ahead of me. I rang the bell and the Rabbi's wife opened the door a crack and in the dark I could only see her in shadow. She said hurriedly, "Go around to the back door."

She let me in, and without looking at me, pointed to the stove. "I forgot to light it before Shabbos," she mumbled. Holding a broom, she stood by the wall as if she were trying to become one with it. I took a wooden match from the box and lit the pilot lights on the burners. "They're lit," I told her, sneaking a glance her way. Her wig was slightly off-center and she turned away from me, but not before I saw her face was bruised on one side. Her lip hung down and her cheek was swollen. She saw me peeking and moved back deeper into the shadows.

"Oven too," she mumbled.

Getting down on my knees in my Shul clothes, I opened the bottom door and lit the oven pilot light. As I was brushing off my knees, I saw the counter with peeled potatoes and carrots, and several chickens lying on a board next to the sink. "Go," she said.

"Mirsky," I said, and ran out of the house heading back to Shul.

Liar

As with many of the women, my Mother left Shul after the first service. She would go home and prepare a cold lunch from the Erev Shabbos leftovers. It would be waiting for my brothers and me when we got home after we changed into our play clothes.

Leaving the Rabbi's house running, I rounded the corner one block from Shul and had to stop before slamming into a group of women. They had the sidewalk blocked and I couldn't cut into the street and go around them because of the parked cars. I could hear them jabbering away as I stopped.

"What are you doing out of Shul?" my mother asked moving to the front of the group. The other ladies stood behind my mother and said nothing. "I was on an errand for the Rabbi," I told her.

"On Shabbos? The Rabbi sent you on an errand? Hah!" my mother said. The other women whispered to each other and shook their heads. "And did this errand cause you to get your Shabbat clothes dirty?"

"Yes," I said. "I have to go back to Shul now," I told her.

"Oh, now you want to go to Shul. Where have you been, tell me?"

"I told you, Mom."

Surrounded by the women who had crept up around my mother, her lips quivering as they do when she's really angry, she asked in a very controlled voice, "And what was this errand for our Rabbi that was so important as to take you out of Shul?"

"He sent me to his house," I said.

"His house?"

"Yes."

"Why did the Rabbi send you to his house?" my Mother asked.

"He needed me to do something for the Rebbetzin," I said.

"What?" she demanded.

I looked down at the sidewalk and pushed a pebble around
with my shoe.

"Well?" she demanded.

"To light the oven for the Rebbetzin," I confessed.

"Light the oven on Shabbos? You are going to stand there
and tell me that you are taking Mr. Farley's place as the Shul's
new Shabbos Goy?", my Mother asked, raising both hands to
her heart.

Her slap across my face sent me into the bushes, where a hole
was ripped in my only suit coat. Tears welled in my mother's
eyes. "Liar! Wait till I get you home!"

I got up and took off running. At the corner, I turned around
to see if she was chasing me. She wasn't. The other women
continued on as one, but my mother, handkerchief in hand,
stood alone waiting for the light to change.

It was after dark when I finally succumbed to hunger and
fatigue and went home to get "what was coming to me". I
immediately went up to the bedroom I shared with my older
brother, Shelley, and changed out of my Shabbos suit, into
dungarees and a polo shirt. Mark, my younger brother, was
sleeping. I walked slowly down the stairs and into the kitchen,
passing the living room where my Mother sat, head in her
hands, talking on the phone. Shelley looked up from his book
and smiled and did a neck slash with his finger. He had
probably been waiting hours for me to come home to get my
beating. There was a plate on the table with a drumstick, a
baked potato, and a mixture of peas and carrots. It wasn't hot
or cold but I ate it down quickly and opened the refrigerator
looking for dessert. I took out a small glass bowl of red Jell-O
and ate it standing. Feeling fortified, I went into the living
room and sat down on the couch. I could feel its springs
pushing into my legs.

"Do you have any idea how much you shamed me in front of
the other women?" My mother grabbed a fistful of her hair in
each hand. Her face was red and wet, her knuckles white.

"Mom. Please don't cry."

"I won't punish you if you tell the truth," she lied.

"This time you should tell Mom the truth," Shelley smiled.

"I did. Why don't you mind your own business?"

She said, "That was Mrs. Levine on the phone, who spoke to Mrs. Cutler, who mentioned to the Rabbi our running into you coming back from his house. The Rabbi said he didn't know what she was talking about."

"There's got to be a mistake, Mom. Geez, that's what happened," I said.

"He's calling the Rabbi a liar, Mom." Shelley was smiling.

"I wish God would take me," my mother pleaded. "I can't handle this anymore. I can't face my neighbors and certainly not the Rabbi."

Mom always knew that her wishing for death was the sure-fire way to bring out the truth and apologies. I said nothing. Shelley smirked at me when Mom wasn't looking. I was going to get a beating and my brother put down his book to watch. "Well?", Mom asked.

"Tell Shelley to stop smirking at me," I said.

Shelley had the book back up by the time my Mother turned towards him.

"Don't change the subject. I asked you a question."

I said nothing.

Mom turned her back and hung her head. "Where did I go wrong? I tried my best to raise you as good, decent kids and what do I get? I get a son who has no shame and can lie with a straight face. I wish I were dead."

"Mom. Don't say that" Shelley said, running over to Mom hugging her. "We need you. Don't wish that." I didn't cry. Shelley crossed his eyes at me.

"Other mothers believe their kids." Kicking the couch until my foot hurt, I said, "I don't care about a Bar Mitzvah anymore."

Stomping out of the room, I wished that my mother would die.

I had my Bar Mitzvah on a Monday with none of my friends there—only a bunch of old men smelling of snuff, my mother, grandfather, my brothers Shelley, and Mark. Shelley didn't want to take off from school, but Mom made him take a half-day. Mark was too young for school. I chanted my Hebrew but didn't make a speech. After the service, there was a bottle of Four Roses brought by my grandfather, a decanter of wine, and some cookies and strudel my Mother baked. I got no presents.

I never got to stand on a chair, after the blessing over the challah and the wine, with all of my friends surrounding me as I tossed out chocolate bars from a box. I had watched all of my friends do that and always got caught up in the excitement of trying to catch more than one and watching the Bar Mitzvah boy toss extra Hershey Bars towards his closest friends and try to keep them from the kids he really didn't like. Standing on the chair tossing out chocolates was the culmination of the ceremony—the part where everyone looked up to you. On my Bar Mitzvah day, no one looked up to me.

My Grandfather shook my hand as did many of the old-timers in the Shul, and they drank shots of Four Roses and ate my Mother's strudel and cookies.

First Funeral

Our mother sent my brother and me to sit next to our father.
"Don't fidget," she said. "He doesn't like fidget."
"He's already upset," I said. "He's sitting alone and crying."
"At least he loved your grandmother," she said.
My older brother (by one year) didn't speak to our father
because he moved and left us. I didn't care because he only
spoke to me to correct me or call me names.
"Mom says we should sit with you."
"Don't talk or fidget," he said.
"Can we breathe and cry?"
His look said it all.
Grandma was in a closed box at the head of the room. The
funeral director, Robert L. Graves, walked from the
anteroom where the family was receiving visitors. The
immediate family entered and took their seats in the front
two rows.
A curtain parted behind grandma and a string quartet played
Russian music. My Aunt Lizzy, the only unmarried sister,
walked over to us and spoke to my father. "Ben, it's not too
late to make amends. Go to Lily."
My father didn't speak.
Director Graves said, "By request of the family". He pushed
a button on the coffin and the top half opened.
I asked my brother if Director Graves was going to saw
Grandma in half.
"Don't be stupid," my father said and got up to get in line to
see grandma in her coffin. We followed him and he stood still
in front for a long time, staring down, and then kissed the
coffin.
My brother and I looked in at grandma and I said, "She looks
real" and my brother said "She is real. Real dead." I reached
in to touch her, and my brother told me touching a dead
person was a sin.
The band played a foxtrot. My father walked over to my
mother and held his hand out. She paused, then took it and

14

they danced beautifully around the coffin, down the aisle, and back to my mother's seat where my father bowed and returned to his seat. My mother always said that for a big man dad was light on his feet. I asked Dad if he felt light on his feet when he danced with Mom. He shot me another look. Director Graves introduced the Rabbi who spoke in Hebrew, English and threw in some Yiddish. He told stories about my grandfather leaving Russia, working, and sending boat tickets for grandma and his parents. Gramps sat, tears running down his cheeks.

None of the seven sisters spoke to each other until they got back to grandpa's house and washed their hands from the pitcher and bowl on the front stoop and then put the food out. Food loosened their tongues and they spoke to each other complimenting each dish, Mr. Graves, and the Rabbi. Dad never showed.

Something in My Eye

Ben got off the bus at a stop before the cemetery, and walked over entering from the side, not wanting his soon-to-be ex-family knowing he didn't own a car anymore. The assembled took their spots around the grave—the casket not yet lowered. The immediate family got the folding chairs—the others stood. The boys were cautioned by their mother to behave. There was a slight hill to the cemetery and Mirsky saw a man standing next to a large, beautifully shaped maple tree. He nudged his older brother and pointed just as their father stepped behind the tree out of sight.

"What?" Shelley asked.

"Dad. Dad's over there behind the tree watching the funeral."

"He watched the funeral at the funeral parlor."

"Well, he's watching what's going on here."

"I don't care. I don't want anything to do with him. I don't want to even look at him."

"What about at the funeral place? You were sitting next to him, and you must have looked over at him."

"No. I was sitting next to you, and you were sitting next to him and I didn't even look at you."

"Not even when we were whispering?"

"Not even."

"How come?"

"Don't talk to me. I want to think about Grandma, not him."

"Why are you crying?"

"Don't be stupid. Why do you think?"

"He's walking over to us."

"Don't tell me about him. Okay?"

"Okay."

"I can smell his aftershave. I'm going on the other side and I'm going to give Grandpa a hug."

"I want to give Grandpa a hug, too."

"Later. You can hug him later. I said it first."

"Said what?"

"Hugs on Grandpa," Shelley said heading over towards Grandpa, Momma, and the aunts sitting, looking straight ahead.

"Where's Shelley going?" the boy's father asked.

"He's going to hug Grandpa."

"Too bad he didn't see me; I could've used a hug."

"He knew you were coming but he wanted to hug Grandpa."

"You can hug me." I said.

"Why? Do you need a hug?"

"Sometimes."

"I thought you said Shelley was going over to Grandpa."

"I did."

"Well, you lied again. He's standing off by himself and he's not near Grandpa," Dad said shaking his head at me.

"I didn't lie. Why are you crying?" I asked.

"I'm not crying. I got something in my eye."

"I'm going to go over and hug Grandpa."

"You can hug me if you want."

"No. I'll save my hug for Grandpa."

"You always have a wiseacre remark—don't you?" his father said and turned away.

"If you say so, Dad."

"Well, I say so. I'm going to talk to Shelley."

"He doesn't want to talk to you," I told him.

"There you go—another lie. What's with the tears?"

"Something in my eye. That's what."

Nudnik

My Uncle Yussel sent me to the store. He told me what he wanted and said I could buy candy with the change.
I got squirrel nuts, Turkish Taffy (strawberry and banana), dots on paper (two feet), fireballs, Milk Duds, chocolate and red Tootsie Pops, chocolate-covered cherries, wax bottles of root beer, and a mini-Mounds Bar.
I told him when I got back, as I held out the candy offering to him, that he didn't give me enough money to get everything on his list.
He told me to tell him what he told me. I said, "You told me to go to the store and get some candy and with the leftover money to get you a pack of Camels, a quart of milk, and the newspaper."
"Shmendrik", he said, "I told you to get Camels, milk, and the newspaper, and to use any money left over to get yourself some candy. Do you remember?"
"I did remember but I started with the candy first. I didn't think it would make a difference."
"Nudnik. Now what do you think?"
"I still think you didn't give me enough money."

Walking Around Money

I needed a job, but you had to be sixteen to get working papers and I was only twelve. Shelley was thirteen and satisfied with the $.25 a week allowance Mom gave us, and Mark was eight and got a dime but usually lost it.
I needed some walking around money. Some Devil Dog and RC Cola money and some cash so I could get in the parking lot blackjack or craps games that sprung up after payday Fridays. I borrowed three bucks from Aunt Lizzie to buy a paper hawking business outside Sikorsky.
I'd ride my bike to the Columbia Market where the Bridgeport Post dropped off their papers for all the kids with paper routes and I'd pick up my bundle but didn't have to roll each paper tight to throw into a yard. I'd put them flat into my canvas bag and ride my bike to Sikorsky and on good days stand outside yelling for people to get their Bridgeport Post and blast, "read all about (insert headline)" and people would sometimes give me a dime instead of a nickel. On rainy or real cold snowy days, I'd go in the building and catch people right after they punched out. There was a group of three ladies who liked to tell me how cute I was and muss my hair. One even kissed me on the cheek.
I was making decent money when the drop-off paper guy said he had an open route in the area and did I want it. I could clear about $15 per week and Shelley told me he'd buy my hawking business, but Mom made me just give it to him.
I expanded the route and delivered for two years and was the first person to slip Christmas cards in the newspaper and pretty soon all the newsboys were doing it. That was good for at least fifty bucks.
Then Burt, the owner of Columbia Market, offered me a job working in his store: cleaning, stacking, whatever needed to be done and I learned a lot. I also got yelled at by my mother for giving up a fifteen dollar plus tips job to take a twelve-dollar job. Since I had to give her half, she was taking a pay cut but she wasn't up for that, so she bumped me up to a $10

give which we fought about constantly. It wasn't long before I learned how to make up the difference in the market. Some, but not much, was legit when I made a delivery—but that was infrequent, and I was still delivering mostly to the Projects or the houses surrounding them.

I liked the idea of learning to be a butcher and was tired of having to get dressed again on snowy or rainy evenings to bring someone a paper I'd missed. And they would call, that's for sure.

I loved wearing the butcher's apron as much as I liked wearing the carpenter's apron that held nails when I worked with my grandfather.

I worked there until the year I turned sixteen and could get a job paying minimum wage of $.85 an hour. It was time. Burt and Betty knew I was taking money on the side but try as they might they could never catch me at it. And as much as I wanted to brag to someone, especially them, I never did.

Columbia Market

I stood next to Burt, his English Leather scent filling my
nostrils as I watched him saw two steaks coated with mold,
and then had me bring the rest of the beef back into the
cooler and hang it on the hook. It was a heavy load for a
thirteen-year-old kid. When I came out, he was scraping the
mold off the steaks into the barrel filled with fat that would
be going to the fat renderer on Friday.
"Nothing is as tender as these steaks will be," he said.
"Maybe I'll call you upstairs and let you taste a piece. They're
aged and when they age, they get moldy."
He told me to scrub the block. I held the wood brush with
the solid metal teeth and pushed it back and forth until it was
white and there was no more sign of blood or meat on the
butcher block, which was worn down in the middle from
years of metal brush cleaning.
Burt and Betty had an apartment upstairs, in the back and the
kitchen overlooked the entrance and a good part of the
narrow store.
"Bring me up garlic and a small onion," he yelled down, and I
did and saw that the table was set for two with nice china and
two glasses of white wine. The steaks were in a fry pan on the
gas range and Burt said, "All you need to cook these perfect
is salt on the pan bottom, and then top it off with butter,
grilled onions and garlic. Smells incredible, doesn't it?"
I heard the bell and went down to the store and sold a loaf of
Wonder bread, a pack of Pall Malls and the lady wanted two
pork chops. I went into the cooler, took out the rack, and
sliced two down to the bone, and then with the cleaver
chopped through for two one-inch-thick chops and weighed
them atop a piece of butcher paper. She watched to see that I
didn't have my thumb on the scale and I didn't—I had it on
the draped butcher paper adding about twenty-five cents to
her chops. She added a can of green beans to her order, and I
added it up on her paper bag and then wrote it on her
running tab.

She left and I returned the rack to the cooler, scrubbed the butcher block down again, and went out from behind the counter where Burt and Betty could see me and straightened some cans and then began sweeping the floor.

"Mirsky, come up here before the steak is all gone."

I didn't want their lousy steak but I was hungry and weak-willed so I climbed the stairs to their apartment and Burt cut off a nickel sized piece of steak and said, "Try a piece of the best." I chewed it and made the right mmm mmm sounds and wanted to run down and make myself a bologna sandwich I was so hungry. "Next time I'll cut a bigger piece so you can have more," he said.

The phone rang and Betty got up to take the call and I went back downstairs, trying to figure out what I could steal and get away with when Betty called me back. "That was your mother—she wants you to bring three hot dogs and two cans of vegetarian beans home for supper tonight."

I only lived around the corner in the projects and we ate mostly casseroles because that's what my mother could afford. I weighed the hot dogs and put their exact weight and cost along with the beans on my mother's tab.

I brought the garbage can of fat out from the cooler and took the fat (for adding to the beef) from the top of the meat grinder for making chopped meat, put it in the can, and brought it back into the cooler. We always kept a supply of fat to add to the chuck steak when someone wanted hamburger. I swept behind the counter and Burt and Betty came down. Burt checked my mother's bag and her tab and Betty gave me a hug and told me to go home to my family. She thought she was making me feel cared for with the hug, but I knew she was really frisking me—I could see it in her eyes as she approached me each evening before I left work.

Cars, Trains, and Smoke Rings

Harvey and me sat on the roof of his building in the projects. We had to shimmy up a tree to the branches and then use them ladder-like to get past the second floor and onto the flat asphalt roof. We watched the cars go by on the turnpike and talked. Sometimes a trucker would look our way and one or both of us would raise our hand yank it down and the trucker would do the same blowing his air horn and then we'd wave to each other. The train tracks are between his building and the turnpike, and we sometimes flatten pennies or bottle caps by laying them on the tracks. We do the whistle movement when the engineer looks our way and usually they blow their whistle and wave and laugh since they're slowing down to pull into the Bridgeport station.

"With all these cars going by on the turnpike and if you think of all the turnpikes and roads in the world, it seems as if they wouldn't miss one measly little car. Don't you think?" I asked Harvey.

"You're hung up on that, Mirsky," Harvey says. "You're only thirteen and can't drive anyway."

"That's beside the point," I say.

Harvey points to a man walking down the street towards the building we're on. "That's the Puerto Rican guy who just moved in. He and his wife live two doors down from me. He comes home every day for lunch. My mother says he gets more than lunch."

We can hear Spanish voices from an open window, and we hurry over and lay down above the bedroom window and lean over, looking in. The guy was on top of his wife humping away, her legs straight up in the air, and she's yelling in Spanish, and all the time her eyes are open and she's chewing gum, looking at us looking at her. Finally, she gives a yell and pounds his back with her fists, and he collapses on her as she pops a bubble.

He rolls off, grabs a cigarette from the pack on the floor, lights up, and lies on his back, and blows smoke rings as she rolls over and puts her arm over his chest. He looks at me and Harvey, our faces upside down, and blows a smoke ring in our direction, and winks.

Corner Store

Ray Hayman was not only tough but crazy. Out of school as much as in—fighting, stealing lunch money, and bagged lunches too. He was lean but muscular and only 5'6" and even the football players kept their distance.

He lived a half dozen buildings over in the projects. His apartment was one on my paper route and every so often when I rang the bell for the weekly payment his mother would tell me to wait, and Ray would come to the door. "Hi Ray," I'd say, "collecting for the paper," and he'd say, "No jingle this week," take the paper, then shut the door and I'd nod and chalk it up to a business expense.

Once, he was inside the corner store playing pinball while a half dozen of us were milling around outside waiting for him to leave so we could play. I was the smallest and the chunkiest. The door opened and the other guys backed away and I said my usual, "Hi Ray" and he said, "Give me a quarter." All I had was a quarter and that was five games, so I shook my head. "Sorry, Ray. No can do," I said.

"I'm gonna kick your ass," he said, lunging head down to butt me in my soft belly, but fear took over and I grabbed the collar of his jacket and pulled it over his head and pushed it down, and kneed him in the face and then, while his zipped-up jacket was still over his head, I punched him with rights and lefts until my hands hurt and when he pulled his jacket back tears were streaming down his face and I knew I was going to get my ass kicked then but he said, "I'm going to tell my mother," and ran off.

Understand, now. I've had fights before and lost almost everyone, but this was different. My friends treated me like a hero and even paid for my first pinball game. Twenty minutes later, housecoat and apron flying, Mrs. Hayman stormed into the store and pointed at me.

"You Porky Pig little sombitch, you had no call to hurt my Raymond. When his brother gets out of prison in two weeks I'm sending him over to slice you up."

I tried to convince my mother we had to move and move quickly. She told me I shouldn't be fighting and if we could move, we wouldn't be living in the projects.

Ray's brother, Roy Albert Hayman, was finally released from prison and his picture was on the Bridgeport Post's front page. He walked to a gas station after the bus dropped him off in some small town and he swiped car keys from a guy who was filling up and then went into the station and knifed the owner, grabbed a pistol. and cleaned out the register. The police showed up after getting a call from the driver who had his keys swiped and was hiding in the phone booth. Roy Albert blasted away at them, hitting one cop in the chest, trying to get to a getaway car but he got shot in the leg and the gun jammed. He dropped it and put up his hands surrendering. He was tackled and beaten bloody and senseless, and never made it home to slice me up and I don't expect he will, so I stopped delivering papers to Ray's house and I never said, "Hi Ray" again not even after his brother went to the electric chair.

Paul Beckman

Columbia Market Delivers

I started up the back stairs with the box of groceries I was to
leave in the kitchen, but the third step squeaked and I froze
and could smell my fear mixed with sweat. I saw a light
through the balustrades and peeked in the open door and saw
a fat, naked man lying on a metal table. His death smell rose
like heat, and it hit me, and I ran up the stairs to the
apartment over the funeral parlor and without knocking, I
opened the door to the kitchen and put the groceries on the
counter, and headed back for the other box.
A stream of smoke cut off my exit and a man asked if I
happened to see a fat, naked, dead man, on the way up. I
starred at Mr. Dichello, and he smiled and asked again, said
he misplaced him, and the smile showed his two gold teeth,
one above the other, shining brightly from the overhead light.
"I'm going down for your other groceries," I said.
"Where's Burt?" he asked.
"He's in the truck waiting for me so I'd better hurry."
"Well, if you see that naked, fat, dead man hold onto him and
give me a yell, willya?"
The Devil Dog came up in my throat. I'd swiped it from the
store and ate it quickly before Burt came down with the
order. "Get two empty boxes and I'll call out the items. You
bring them over and I'll pack em up and you can come with
me to Dichello's to deliver them."
I ran down the stairs and didn't look back at the naked, fat,
dead guy on the table and was sweating and shaking when I
got to the truck.
"You look like you've seen a ghost," Burt laughed. "Bring
this other box up quick so we can deliver the rest of the
groceries."
As soon as the back door closed behind me, I stuck my head
in the box and breathed in the fresh seeded rye bread. I
sucked in the smell afraid I'd suck the seeds out. Finally, I
lifted my head and took the stairs two at a time barely
glimpsing the naked, dead, fat man's feet.

27

Kiwi

My mother stood at the kitchen counter unlumping the mashed potatoes. I leaned nearby waiting to lick out the pan. She said, "Reuven, you can do anything with your life that you choose to. You have the brains. You can be anybody and do anything you want. Just remember that." I didn't want to listen but I wanted that mashed potato bowl.

This was the usual lecture that I got around report card time when my brother brought home straight A's. "I'm not comparing the two of you," she would say, comparing the two of us, "you are both different people. But, if he can do it so can you. The difference between a B and an A is just a little effort. It's not that you don't have the ability, but you don't show the effort."

"Yes mom," I said dutifully.

"Anything is possible if you work hard and get good grades. Your brother wants to study science. There's a lot of prestige in being a scientist. There's also probably a lot of money in science."

"Mom," I said. "I don't want to be a scientist."

"You have plenty of time to decide. Just get the grades."

"Mom, I know what I want to be when I grow up."

"What's that?"

"I want to be a shoe salesman."

Mom didn't miss a mash but glared at me. "Get serious," she said.

"Mom, I am serious."

"Well then, don't be stupid."

"Stupid? What do you mean by stupid? What's stupid about being a shoe salesman?"

Mr. Kleinman was our shoe salesman and the nicest man in the world. Even mom would say that after we went shopping for our school shoes. He would take the time to measure our feet, ask about baseball, tell us jokes and flip us a Snickers bar from the box he kept behind the register. He was the neatest guy and my brother and I looked forward to our yearly shoe trip to see him.

"You have no ambition," Mom says.

My brother Shelley tells her that he wants to be an astro-physicist specializing in molecular anti-matter and my mother looks proud and gives him cookies before dinner. All A's, Shelley is ten, still wets the bed, doesn't have to study, and tortures the cat.

I have a B+ average, a paper route, watch the seven o'clock news, eat with utensils and my mother calls me stupid because I want to be a shoe salesman.

She doesn't realize how good the smell of new leather is. And to be able to savor it every day instead of just once a year on school shoe day would make me the luckiest guy in the world. I wonder if Mr. Kleinman became a shoe salesman because of his love of the smell of leather. I can't wait until I can hold a person's foot in one hand and gently guide it into a shoe with the aid of a shoehorn. Then I will twirl the shoehorn around my finger twice and pop it in my back pocket. That will be my trademark – a double twirl.

In the bathroom mirror I practice my lectures on the use of shoe trees. Not only do I polish my shoes every day, but I have several different speeches, all geared to selling on the benefits of each kind of shoe polish. My favorite shoe polish is Kiwi Oxblood which many people confuse with Kiwi Cordovan. Oxblood has a slightly rosier tint to it, a little livelier, and they can actually be interchanged without hurting the leather. We only have the adjustable shoe trees right now, but when I'm older I plan to have a set of wooden ones for each pair of shoes in my wardrobe.

I watched Mr. Kleinman last week from the window outside his store. He motioned me in, as he so often does, and then he got busy trying to sell a very pretty lady a pair of shoes. He must have scattered more than a dozen boxes of shoes all around and finally she picks up a pair of black pumps and Mr. Kleinman holds her foot, and she tries to push it into the shoe. Even with the shoehorn, it's not going anywhere and

Mr. Kleinman turns to me and says, "Reuven, go in the storeroom and get me a pair of these in size seven willie." He winks when the lady turns her head to see who he is talking to.

In no time at all I find the style but there are no seven wides, just seven normal so I bring him a pair of seven and a half willies and hand him the box, so the size is away from the lady. She tries them on, and they glide right on her foot. She puts the other one on and walks around the store and says to Mr. Kleinman, "Size seven, what did I tell you? I'll take them." He winks at me again and I start picking up the other shoes and re-boxing them. While he's ringing up the sale, I put the shoes back in the storeroom.

The lady leaves and Mr. Kleinman flips me a quarter and says, "You're a natural, Reuven."

I smile and run out of the shoe store and down to the Crystal Palace Pinball Arcade where I get a Pepsi and a handful of nickels and plan to spend the afternoon trying to win free games. It was on my second game when Mr. Dobieski caught me with the legs of the pinball machine resting on my toes and tossed me out of the Palace. "That's a one-week suspension!" he yelled. "Next time it'll be permanent." I still had thirty cents left so I went to the Strand Theater and for two bits I saw two Hopalong Cassidy's, a newsreel, three days' worth of previews, and two spooky pictures that gave me nightmares for a week. On my way home I spent my last nickel on a yellow box of Chiclets and chewed them all at the same time.

Headache Pads

I wandered into the house around six-thirty just as my
mother felt the need to take a swing at someone. "I'll teach
you to stay out all night," she said as she slapped me across
the side of my head. I didn't argue with her cause I didn't
want to get hit again, so I started for my room to get away.
"Just a minute, young man. I spent my time cooking, and
you can damn well sit down and eat, but it's cold, and I'm not
warming it up."
"Yes, Mom," I said. I started to eat, and she said, "Don't we
wash our hands anymore before eating? I've got half a mind
to send you to bed with no supper." I wish she'd make up her
half mind. I really didn't care whether I ate or not – I just
wanted to go upstairs and polish my wing tips, they were
scuffed from the pinball machine legs resting on them.
"May I go and wash my hands?" I asked standing and
pushing the chair from the table.
"Why ask me? You seem to do just as you please anyway,"
my mother said.
I figured that it didn't matter to her, so I sat down and picked
up the cold chicken with my hands and my mother got up
and stood over me shaking with rage. "You never learn, do
you? Go to bed this instant," she commanded. "And don't let
me catch you polishing your shoes, or you'll really get what
for."
It wasn't my fault that Dad left town with a Polish cleaning
lady, and everybody knew it. It also wasn't my fault that I was
the spitting image of him. Mom always says that I walk his
walk, whistle his whistle, laugh his laugh, and snicker just like
him. I wasn't copying him; I hadn't seen him since I was little
so how could I be blamed? I did everything I could to be
good, but Mom looked at me and saw Dad, and when she
saw Dad, she saw fire and when she saw fire I usually got my
butt kicked.
I just got under the covers when I heard Mom yell, "Reuven!
Get down here and go to the store for me!"

"I'm in bed Mom," I yell back. "Send Shelley."

"Are you coming down or am I coming up?"

"Right there, Mom," I said, dressing as fast as I could.

When I got downstairs Mom handed me a note folded in half and said, "I've got a terrible headache. Give this note to the man at the corner store and he'll give you headache pads. Hurry back and don't play pinballs." I took the money and ran down to the store hoping to have time to get in one game of pinball, but there was someone playing and another guy with his nickel on the machine waiting his turn. I watched for a couple of minutes and then walked over to the counter and reached in my pocket for the note to give to Ralph. It wasn't there. Frantically I searched every pocket twice.

"What are you looking for?" asked Ralph, and I told him that my mother had given me a note and I lost it. "What did it say?" he asked, and I told him I didn't read it but that she had a headache and wanted a box of headache pads. I'd gotten them before with notes from home. "What the hell are headache pads?" he asked, and I pointed to the blue and white boxes on the top shelf behind him and he asked me if I was for real. "Mirsky, you're nine-years old. You should know what these things are for. Right guys?" he said to the pinball crew. They walked over as Ralph told them my story and then laughed as he explained to me what headache pads really were.

Angry and embarrassed I took my time walking home, kicking a can all the way. When I finally walked in Mom opened her mouth to yell at me and I thought about throwing the bag at her and running up to my room or running away but decided that the last thing in the world I needed was another beating. So, I handed her the Kotex and her change and turned to go back to bed.

"Reuven, go eat your meal. I heated it up," Mom said softly. "I'll be in to join you in a minute."

Paul Beckman

In Those Days They Knew How to Have a Parade

The Fourth of July parade begins in Bridgeport's North End follows Park Avenue South under the turnpike under the railroad track overpass past the projects we live in and ending in Seaside Park where the Barnum and Bailey Circus is waiting. Mom wakes us at 4am to put blankets on the curb and we have to sleep on them to protect our float-watching turf since last year we left out our kitchen chairs and went home to sleep. The chairs were missing, and we got a beating, something we were used to, but didn't believe we had it coming.

Our Bodies Red and Sore

As soon as the movie was over my brother, and I had to run into our father's office in the theater he managed. Once there we had to strip down to our underpants and he'd take a large bottle of Old Spice from his desk drawer, sit smugly in his big chair, and sprinkle it all over us and rub it in—hair and all. Then we'd get dressed and he'd shake it over our clothes, collect the money from the ticket takers and candy girl and lock it away in the safe and then lock up the theater.

Then he'd drive us home to our mother and the projects. We would be hungry and fearful of our mother's reaction to "his" smell permeating us. It was nothing new. We'd have to undress outside on the back porch and Mom would throw our clothes in the wringer washer. Then we'd run inside and get in the tub where Mom would scrub our father out of us as best, she could, all the while complaining about him doing this to annoy her and why did we let him.

After we soaked and the water turned cold Mom would come in and sniff us and if we passed the sniff test, we could put on our pjs and go to the kitchen table for supper. If we didn't pass the sniffs, it was back for another Ivory soap scrubbing until our bodies were red and sore and Mom would make us wait for dinner while she scrubbed our father out of the tub.

Who Can I Tell?

My mother sent me upstairs to take a bath before dinner. After I ran the water, I saw there was a hole in the wall over the rim of the tub looking into our neighbor's tub. I saw the mother from next door climb into the tub, turn on the shower, and begin soaping her breasts and between her legs with a washcloth. She saw me watching her and yelled at me to scoot or she'd tell my mother. I didn't scoot and she didn't tell my mother that night or the next three nights I watched her before the wall was fixed.

Lessons from My Father

My father talked in "sayings"— trying to work at least one into every conversation.

"There is no good time for something bad to happen," he said for the umpteenth time while I stood in front of him crying over an injustice.

Tired, really tired, of his lack of sympathy and verbal abuse, I stomped on his bare foot with the hard rubber cleats I was still wearing from baseball. While he was doubled over on the shag carpet trying to rub out the pain, I asked, "Wouldn't a better time for that to have been when you were wearing shoes?"

Later that evening he walked into my bedroom, grabbed my baseball bat, and said, "It might have been a better time, but it certainly wouldn't have been a good time." Then, swinging my bat like a crazy man he trashed my room and said, "All's well that ends well."

He smiled at me cowering in the corner before walking out.

Cruel Choices

I looked both ways and then rode my bike down one curb
and jumped the curb across the street, heading for Angelo's
Pear Tree Shop and a nice cool lemon ice in a paper cup I
could suck on afterwards. I turned the corner and saw my
mother at the same time she saw me. I was ten and being
punished and not allowed off our block for another week. My
mother wasn't supposed to be hugging Uncle Morris, much
less kissing him. Our eyes connected and we both looked
away.
I had a decision to make—either turn around and go back to
my block and give up the lemon ice or try to ride past my
mother and uncle and make it to the store.
Either way, I knew I was going to be in for it.

I Make Mom Fume

Sunday will be here before I know it my mother said.
How can that be I asked?
Because it's like that every week she said.
But if you know your days of the week by the time it's
Saturday you'll know that Sunday will be the next day and
that won't be before you know it.
You have an answer for everything, don't you, she said.
You're just like him and she turned back to reading the
newspaper.

My Uncle's Secret Project

I spent the weekend at my Uncle Carl's house. While I mowed the lawn, he was busy in his workshop on some secret project. I finished with that sharp-bladed push mower a little after noon and my aunt called me in for lunch. She made tuna burgers on hamburger rolls with thick slices of tomato and the great, from the can, onion rings. That and a grape soda was my favorite lunch.

My uncle had me wait at the table while he brought something upstairs. He'd made me a rifle with a wood stock, bent nail trigger and a two-foot pipe barrel. He told me it was similar to the rifle he had in Korea. What a day!

On my seventeenth birthday, my uncle told me to bring the rifle over. He drilled me in his backyard like I was in basic training, and he was my boot camp Sergeant. It felt real and never like a game especially since he wore his uniform while training me. He went over marching, saluting, turning to instructions, and shouldering the rifle. He wanted me to be ready if I was drafted and he wanted me to have a heads up on becoming a boot camp Colonel and getting my first stripe.

The week after graduation I had a family going away party and the next day I left for basic training. Four weeks later I was promoted to Corporal of boot camp training following the same instructions that I'd practiced in my uncle's yard. After graduation, we all sat around waiting for our assignments. I got called to the base commander's office and told I'd be working as a permanent drill instructor, but I hemmed and hawed and told the Colonel I wanted to carry a rifle and join the 101st Division but I landed a forward air controller gig which was the closest position to the 101st. I took the stripe to sew on, snapped to attention, and left proud as could be even four months later as I lay in the hospital bed with a pair of bullet wounds in my leg from my first jump in country.

The Project Olympics are Not for the Faint of Heart

I'm in the Project Olympics, signed up to be a hurdler, when the gun goes off and the kid next to me keels over and blood is squirting from his neck, I take off and I look behind me and there's a flock of cops in uniform chasing us hurdlers and my fellow runners are ahead of me and they're all wearing double-breasted suits, wide, hand-painted ties, fedoras, and spit-shined Florsheims and I look at myself in a window and I'm wearing the same and then we come to the first fence and since it's only three feet off the ground we all hurdle it but being last I hit a button after I do and a traffic light turns to red and the cops come to a stop as we continue.

My brother and I are sitting on the stoop playing 500 rummy with the cops and robbers running by and he says how much he'd like to be a cop and wear a uniform and I tell him I want to wear a double-breasted suit and Florsheim's and he deals and tells me that he's special because he can dream in color and I can't but he's all smug and I tell him I dream in black and white but it's 3D and he says prove it and I say you prove I don't.

We stop playing and take a walk and see two rabbis playing hopscotch and across from them is a wrestling ring and there's an all-nun tag-team match going on and I sense something isn't right. I yell over and try to get the rabbis and the nuns to change positions, but they all attack me for getting in their business. Embarrassed, my brother goes back home.

So now I'm falling again and look around and my legs are attached to a bungee cord, and I see nothing and no one until my mother steps out of a cloud and gives me the look and hands me a helmet.

I'm walking around the Bronx Botanical garden and a guard walks over to me and tells me if I want to stay I have to remove both the bungee cord and the helmet which I do. I ask him where the cactus exhibit is and he says I'm a guard, not a tour guide now get out of here and he hands me back my helmet, straps it on and rehooks me up to the bungee. I'm getting hungry and there are chain restaurants all around so I maneuver over to the Pancake House and walk in but they toss me for not having a shirt or shoes and there happens to be a shirt and shoes stand where I get what I need and put it on my credit card and I'm asked by a teen-age boy wearing a Hello My Name is Acne sticker if I'd like table or counter and before I can answer he tells me if I take a table I can have a coupon so I do and I pick up the menu and it only has two items a short stack and a tall stack and I notice the coupon's for the tall stack so I order that and I get a four-foot high stack of pancakes with one butter pat and a garden hose that says maple syrup. The gun goes off and I start eating and I look up just as Hello My Name is Acne gets hit in the arm by the starter's gun bullet and goes down.

Now I hear my mother yelling at me to take a nap and she shoves a cumulous cloud underneath me and tosses a cumulous pillow down and I nap and I'm watching The Jazz Singer with Al Jolson and it's in color but not 3D.

I wake up in time to look down and see my house and yard and the cumulous cloud dissipates and I'm heading straight for my koi pond and execute a belly flop knocking all the koi out of the water and sore as I am I go to them and start apologizing and I grab the big gold one with the black streak and he shakes me off and says "C'mon guys—there's better ponds for us fish," and they stand up on their little fish feet and walk off and I'm thinking ingrates all since I've been feeding them for years now so when the herons come by I point my finger at them walking into the next yard.

My mother comes out and asks where the hell I've been since she's been holding up dinner so I go in and change and when I come out my mother's talking to the wrestling nuns, the four judges are at the bar (and it's not a cash bar) and the herons are sitting on top of the raw bar eating shrimp—the cops are pinning Olympic medals on the crooks and my brother Shelley is arguing the Torah with the rabbis and winning.

Loser

Little League Year 1

Along with my brother we made our way to Wagner Field for
little League tryouts. Shelley was going to pitch on whichever
team we played on, and I had no idea where I'd play.
Coach split us boys into two teams and asked each one what
position we wanted to play. When he got to me I shrugged
and he told me we didn't have a shrug position so pick one or
sit out. I looked down and saw the catcher's equipment and I
pointed to it. Did you ever catch before and I nodded my
head for my first lie.
I was a scared to get hit by the swinging bat, so I didn't get
close enough until the coach who was also the ump kept
kicking me in the butt. I didn't have a strong arm and when I
threw the ball back to Shelley on the mound. I couldn't reach
him, and he had to walk off the mound to get the ball
muttering what a loser I was.
Little League Year 2
I could almost reach Shelley on the mound but not quite, so
he'd walk two or three steps towards me, and most, but not
all of the time, I'd get the ball to him on a fly.
Little League Year 2 second half
I could finally reach Shelley with almost every throw.
Little League Year 3
This was the first year that base-stealing was allowed but
every runner stole second because I couldn't throw that far.
Finally, with a runner on first and us close to winning our
first game, Shelley walked off the mound and called me over.
Listen loser, he said to me, I don't plan on losing this game
so don't even try to reach second base on a throw—stand up
and throw me the ball as hard as you can and I'll fire it to
second and get the runner out trying to steal second. I
nodded.
The batter hit a foul ball and Shelley turned his back to me
and motioned a couple of players to shift to their left. The

ump slapped a fresh ball in my glove and I stood and threw it hard to Shelley and caught him, as he was turning towards home, on the side of his head right above his ear and concussed him.

###

Little League following the beaning of Shelley.

Shelley couldn't play anymore that year. My throw scrambled something in his head, but the good news was the coach talked to me about how much power I had throwing from a standing position instead of from a squat. I became the baseball player in our family that year, and Shelley was offered the batboy position which he happily took.

Pay Day in the Projects c.1959

Eileen's mother sat outside the front door in a kitchen chair when the line began to form at 5pm. One at a time the men and boys handed her a dollar and walked in, looked in wonder and want as her blonde fifteen-year-old daughter opened her blouse and let them ogle her unfettered woman's breasts until the rap on the door signaled time and they left out back where the others were gathered. Eileen bummed smokes and looked at the men looking at her as she posed in the ways her mother taught her. Some returned later that night for Eileen's mother.

A Boy Sees His Plan as Reasonable and Viable

When my mother came home from work I was lying on the couch reading comics while my brothers sat at the kitchen table doing their homework.

Before she asked, I told her I did my homework in study period.

"Liar," she said.

But this time I told her the truth and thankfully she acted towards me like she always did. I walked up the stairs as she yelled after me that I wasn't too big to get slapped around by her.

I brought my math, history, and English books down and lay them on the kitchen table with my homework questions and answers. Mom said, "Do you think that doing your homework one day makes up for all the other days?"

"What would it take to do something right in your eyes?" I asked.

"More. A lot more and watch your mouth, mister," she said. That's when I told her I wanted to move out and go live with her brother and his family.

"Go. Good riddance," she said, and back up the stairs I went and packed my stuff in the family suitcase and lugged it downstairs. I left it by the front door and went into the kitchen and made two peanut butter and banana sandwiches and added an apple to the bag.

"I need bus money," I said, and my mother walked out the back door and lit up a Raleigh. I could see her shoulders shake while she blew smoke rings. I looked at my brother and he looked daggers back at me. I took a quarter from my mother's purse and walked out of the projects to the bus stop hoping my uncle would take me in.

Paul Beckman

The Only Hope of the Jews

You're sitting on your stoop thinking how much you hate the stoop, the building you live in with six side-by-side apartments (now called townhouses), and the neighborhood. You hate the neighborhood because all of the stoops in all of the buildings and all of the wire fenced-in tiny yards smaller than a jail cell look exactly alike and at fourteen-years-old you can't wait to get out of these projects and scrub off the stigma and live in a place where you don't need the roach exterminator every month and head lice aren't the main pets for the little kids and on top of it all your family are the only Jews in Marina Village.
There are lots of blacks and Puerto Ricans (who are mortal enemies) and plenty of white ethnics—Jew-haters from eastern European families.
You look to your left and you see a couple of older and bigger kids coming down the walk and you reach behind you and grab the rock that you scraped against the cement stoop to create jagged edges that makes your fist a weapon and you don't care how big or how many Jew-haters there are you will go after them. Rock in hand you'll punch them repeatedly until they subdue you and "teach you a lesson". You know you'll never learn your lesson and when your mother comes home she'll take one look at you and punish you for fighting and you never tell her you're the only hope of the Jews and she thinks you've gotten to be a ruffian since you had to move to this neighborhood and that, unlike your brother, you're hanging out with the wrong crowd. You take your punishment from her and dream of owning a car and driving as far away from that stoop as you can and never having to carry a jagged rock in your pocket again. And all these years later you still carry the same jagged rock.

47

Yosemite Sam

Lily, still wearing her homemade blue and green housecoat took down her Ouija board from the top of the refrigerator and opened the cabinet that held the drinking glasses. With the Ouija board on the counter, she selected eight glasses and put them on the board. Not being able to bear an open door she quickly closed the glasses door before picking up her board, tray like, and moved around the apartment. The board was well worn from being used as not only a Ouija board and as a tray for her evening glass ritual but also as a tray to bring the kids food when they were sick in bed. She never asked Ouija if it liked being used as a tray—the thought never entered her mind.

Yosemite Sam and Tinker Bell were placed on the sash top of the kitchen window. In the dining room went Tweety Bird, and a Yahrzeit glass, while The Roadrunner, Sylvester, the three little pigs and a chipped jelly glass with a grinning Mickey Mouse went on the sash top of the two windows in the living room.

Lily placed the Ouija board on the kitchen table and dragged a chair over to the door and propped the chair back under the doorknob. She did the same with her front door. Now that her alarm was set for the night, Lily turned on the water kettle and dealt herself a hand of solitaire. She played two games before the water boiled and she got up, made a cup of instant coffee, put the cards away and took out two milk crackers, and sat down at the Ouija board to complete her nightly pre-bed ritual.

As the steam rose from the coffee, Lily put her fingers on the planchette lightly and being a person of habit asked silently the first of the three mandatory questions. "Will I ever marry again?" And then "Did Ben ever love me?" And lastly "Am I ever going to know happiness again?"

Lily's planchette had a space for a pencil where the answers could be written on paper, but she preferred to use it as a wedge and let it lead her to yes or no answers. As always, all three questions pointed her to NO. The planchette only moved slightly but the tip pointed cross board at NO and that was enough for Lily. She put the board away and took her coffee into the living room, turned on the radio softly so as not to wake the children, and lit up a cigarette. She pulled the coupon from beneath the cellophane of the now empty pack and added it to her collection in the end table drawer, where the Raleigh catalogue was also kept. Lily wasn't sure what she was saving up for but knew she had over a thousand coupons elastic banded in packs of a hundred. Not for a minute did she think of the health aspects of a thousand coupons; but every once in a while, she would add up the cost of buying that many packs or cartons of cigarettes and think about what she could be doing with the money.

Lily fantasized about walking into the Raleigh Coupon store, ignoring the cases and shelves filled with shiny new household appliances, knick-knacks and the like and saw herself standing in line at the cashier's window. "Here," she said when her turn came. "I'd like to exchange these coupons for the money I spent." She pushed the coupons towards the cashier who pulled down the iron bar window gate blocking the coupons path and said, "Sorry. I'm closing for my break. You'll have to come back another time." This fantasy scene never changed and Lily never ever got to imagine what it would be like to have a few hundred dollars at her disposal. She couldn't even allow herself the luxury of having a good fantasy.

In the morning, before her boys woke, Lily put the chairs and glasses away, checking to see with her practiced eye if anything had been moved during the night. Yosemite Sam was out of place. She knew there was no way she would have put him on the same side of the window lock as Tinker Bell. At breakfast, she interrogated her boys. It wasn't much of an interrogation, Reuven said he came downstairs to get a drink of water and grabbed Yosemite, took his drink, and put Yosemite back. Lily, angry beyond reason, yelled at him for touching her alarm and offered several different scenarios of

what burglars do to children when they break into a house.
Reuven, instead of apologizing or sitting mutely as the others
did or would, told his Mother that Yosemite was his glass,
and he was thirsty and the only other glasses in the cupboard
were Yahrzeit glasses, and he wasn't about to drink out of
one of them.

Lily walked into the kitchen, opened Reuven's lunch bag, and
took out the oatmeal raisin cookie—his favorite, and refolded
the bag, and said nothing more about the alarm as she sent
her boys off to school, lunch bags in hand.

My Only Christmas Story

Dad was coming over to give us presents from Santa. Mom told us he didn't buy them—he got them from his Christmas party at work.

Dad went up to the bathroom which was at the top of the stairs. I was excited after I opened my one present—a Roy Rogers cap pistol. My older brother showed me how to load it. I wanted to tell Dad how much I loved this because I loved Roy Rogers.

I stepped onto the landing waiting for him to come out of the bathroom. The door was open, and I could see him standing sideways, peeing. He turned and saw me looking up at him. "You sneaky little bastard," he yelled.

Scared, I ran and sat next to my brother and his jigsaw puzzle.

The toilet flushed and then angry stomping down the stairs. I kept my head down as he called me a wicked, evil little boy. "Now give the gun to your brother—you lost it for being a sneak." I got up and ran into the dining room with it and he followed yelling at me. Mom walked out of the kitchen and stood with her arms folded.

Dad stopped yelling and stared. I fired two caps at him, and he turned and walked to the front door. He looked around and mom had moved in front of me to block him off. I reached around her and fired two more caps and he stormed out of the house.

Kosher Soap

My wife thinks it's funny that I won't allow Kosher Soap in our house. I don't think it's funny and I tell her so, but she finds reason to bring up this minor issue often amongst friends, and last year they got together and gave me a six-pack of Kosher Soap at my surprise fortieth birthday party.

I looked around the room at their laughing faces and did the only sensible thing I could do—I climbed into a bottle of Knob Creek Bourbon and sipped my way to oblivion during the evening party. The last thing I remember, and it is foggy mind you, is being carried to my bed, stripped to my underwear, and having the Kosher Soap dumped on and around me.

Here are the reasons I give for not allowing this heinous soap into my house: We don't have a kosher house, it smells terrible, it works no better than any other soap, I don't like the brick-like feel and look of it and besides that; "No" is enough of a reason.

No one knows the real reason except my brothers and since I have the goods on them in other areas they keep this to themselves although they are asked all too often.

When I was growing up, I was probably like most other kids, given to telling little lies or making up stories about things once in a while, and when caught my mother would always threaten to wash my mouth out with Kosher Soap if I ever lied to her again. Never Ivory or Palmolive but the Kosher Soap that lay in a dish next to the sink.

I was seven and playing with my friend Doris who was eight and lived next door in our garden apartments. One day we were sitting around our yard by the swings talking and making up names for our neighbors and she offered to let me see what she had under her underpants if I showed her what I had underneath mine. It seemed perfectly reasonable as we stood facing each other with our underpants dropped to our ankles when my mother rounded the corner and saw us.

She yelled at us to pull our pants up and for Doris to go home and tell her mother what she was just doing, and my mother grabbed my arm, quite roughly and dragged me into the house through the living room past my two brothers who were playing a card game and into the kitchen.

She asked what we were doing, and I told her the truth that Doris had made the suggestion and Mom called me a liar and said she was going to teach me a lesson. She grabbed a kitchen chair, put it in front of the sink, turned the water on, and told me to stand on the chair. I made a break for the door, and she caught me and carried me crying to the chair and grabbed the dreaded bar of Kosher Soap and ran it under the water to lather it up. She yelled for my brothers to come and watch what happens when you lie to your mother and then she shoved the Kosher Soap bar into my mouth working it around and pulled it out and put her hand in and swished the soap suds around in every crevice possible. I was sent to bed with no supper and tried to wash the taste out of my mouth and brush it out with toothpaste and all I did was bring it back to the surface,

Now if that's not enough of a reason to keep that crap out of my house than I don't know what is. When my mother died I told her as I stood in front of the casket, head bowed lips moving in barely a whisper, that even though she took the easy way out from my getting back at her I wasn't letting her off the hook. I had both hands on the casket and spent longer than my brothers saying their goodbyes. Little did they know the cause of my tears.

Whenever I visit the cemetery, which is not often but usually for the funeral of another relative, I do like the rest of my family—I walk around visiting my grandparents and other relatives. I carry a few nips with me and have a shot of schnapps with three or four of my favorites which entails my opening the bottle toasting with love and then after my sip, I pour the remainder on the grave to share and leave the bottle on top of the gravestone as my mark.

Stopping by my mother's grave is different. No alcohol for her but I put a chunk of Kosher Soap on her memorial stone hoping that the next rain will wash it down into her final resting place and I pray to God that some of the soap will find its way beneath the soil and through what remains of the casket and into her mouth or whatever is left of it. I'm sure it happens because I see it happening in my mind's eye.

No Tchotchkes for Tanta Trudy

Dear Family,

As of this date I would like you all to begin referring to my
mother as Tanta Trudy instead of Aunt Trudy, Trudy, or hey
Trude. Since the passing of Tanta Yetta earlier this year our
family has been without a Tanta. Tanta—a word that
connotes the first among equals and shows wisdom,
generosity, and commands respect for her place in the family.
Since my mother is now the eldest daughter of all her sisters
the mantle rightfully falls on her shoulders and who better to
take up this position?

Having spoken to several of you, I know that you agree it's
time to make it official. Understand now, my siblings and I
do not expect her sisters or brothers to call her Tanta, but it
would be only right to use the term when speaking of her, as
has been the case with the late New York Tantas—Rhea,
Pearl, Bessie, and Yetta.
We, my brother, sister, and I, want you to know we mean no
disrespect to any of our other loving aunts, but this family has
been too long without a Tanta and Tanta Trudy has agreed to
step up to the plate and fill this void.

In the spirit of family unity that our family is known for there
will be a Welcome Tanta Trudy picnic at one of the cousin's
houses. I'll let you know which cousin in my next letter, but
the date will be Labor Day so save the date.

As you are all aware, it is only proper to welcome in a new
Tanta with a gift, so instead of each of you bringing a
tchotchke that Tanta Trudy will have to dust, we have
decided that a new 70-inch curved screen smart television,
picture in picture, would be the perfect gift.

Please send your donations to me as soon as possible so we can surprise Tanta Trudy before her party. If there is any money left over, we will use it to buy Tanta Trudy a new comfortable lounger to use in front of her new TV.

Sincerely,
Cousin Marvin and siblings

In the Tenderloin

I had an aunt and uncle in San Francisco I'd never met. They were my father's siblings, but while I never communicated with him, I kept up some correspondence with them. Aunt Edith sent me letters and her brother, my Uncle Lou, a Merchant Marine, sent me stamps, coins, and postcards from the world ports he traveled to. Every time he left San Francisco for a trip he'd write me a letter about what he hoped to see and upon his return, he'd write another telling me what he saw. I always asked if they were coming to Connecticut where their mother lived but the question went unanswered.

Edith said I could stay with her on my week's leave from my next base on the Oregon border. She was a social worker who lectured me daily about getting girls pregnant, but I was a nineteen-year-old virgin and shy around girls to boot.

I kept asking to see my Uncle Lou, but she kept putting me off.

Finally, I packed my duffle and said goodbye and told her I called the local Merchant Marine Office and they promised to help me. She caved and told me I was making a mistake, but she'd take me. I didn't know if there was really a local Merchant Marine Office.

We met Uncle Lou at a Tenderloin area bar next to the hotel he was living in. Shot and beer 50 cents.

He was short with a large beer gut, needed a shave, a haircut, and some clean clothes, but I was happy to see him and surprised him with a hug. I watched Edith pass him some bills under the table. She wasn't discrete, she wanted me to see. I told him how much his letters and presents meant to me and I still had all the stamps and coins from foreign places. After the next round Edith said we had to leave, and Lou asked me to wait while he got something from his room. "I'll go with you," I said, and Edith said "No," and grabbed my arm.

I pulled loose and got his room number from the desk clerk. His room was cell-like with a sink filled with water and a bottle of wine floating in it. He handed me a Merchant Marine manual he said he'd been saving for me. I told him he'd always been my hero and I'd like to spend a day together without Edith. He was hesitant and told me he was shipping out the following week and he'd write me when he got back. I hugged him goodbye and kissed him on the cheek and told him I loved him.

Once on the elevator, I lost it. I began crying, expecting my Uncle Lou to be dapper in his Merchant Marine uniform. I punched and kicked the elevator walls—sorry for him, not me. Spent, I turned and hit the down button and my uncle was looking through the elevator window at me and we could see each other's heads disappearing.

Back in the bar, Edith said Lou wasn't shipping out—he was only allowed to clean the boats that came into port and no longer allowed to be an engineer. I told her that he told me he'd been a drug addict and kicked the habit with booze. "A bum," she said. "He's only a bum."

The Last Person in Panik

Father Panik Village in Bridgeport, Connecticut, the worst of the worst in the failed projects experiment was scheduled to be demolished and I wanted to see my old home one last time. I'm not sure why but we only lived there for two years before moving to Marina Village. It was gloomy then and gloomy still when I arrived. Razor wire fences across from Panik, for two long desolate blocks, shielded the closed factories that spewed their pollution into the river they faced. All the buildings were shuttered with large For Sale signs nailed to them.

The police had stopped patrolling it on a regular basis years earlier for fear of getting shot. There was no official gang but other gangs from different parts of town and other projects learned long ago not to enter. Drug sales took place in the open. Now the windows of the vacant units were boarded, graffiti was everywhere. I drove on to the parking lot where we huddled to shoot craps or play blackjack. Yet, good memories and bad.

The people who were being made to move protested about being thrown out of the only home some had ever known. Many were third-generation Father Panik people. In place of the ninety apartments, the city was going to build ten small houses that would go by lottery to dispossessed families.

I drove the parameter and then cut through the side streets slowly seeing for the last time the ugliness of these three-story brick buildings once vibrant with kids playing and the aged and unemployed sitting around smoking and playing tonk for pennies. I saw the triangle of concrete where we held our whiffle ball games, and our kick the can tourneys but I heard that stopped when the drug dealers started claiming sections as their "offices".

I saw a young girl leaning against a building and I pulled to the curb. I walked over to her and said, "Hi. You've got to be the last person in Panik."

I offered her a stick of gum. She took two and said, "One's for later."

"How come you're still here? What are you fifteen, sixteen?"

"Fourteen and my man told me to stay here till he calls for me."

"How long ago was that?"

"Couple of days."

"Hungry?"

She didn't answer, but her look said yes.

"C'mon. We'll go to the Hot Top Diner and get a good meal. Have you back in no time."

She tentatively walked to my car and got in. I drove towards the diner when she said, "Ella."

"Pretty name."

"My momma liked Ella Fitzgerald."

"I'm Mirsky," I said. "What would you like to eat? Hot Top okay?"

"No. No. He'll be at the diner. I'd like a Happy Meal."

We went through the drive-through and Ella didn't order a Happy Meal. She asked if she could order extra for later and I said sure, and she ordered enough for three grown-ups and ate fries all the way to Seaside Park where I stopped the car facing the water and took out my own small bag of fries and a Coke.

"Do you live with your parents?" I asked her.

She didn't answer.

"Where are you going to go when they bulldoze Panik?"

She shrugged and that's how our meal went. I told her there were places that would take her in and send her to school. Places that were clean and she'd have friends and her own room, but she didn't respond.

Finally, she folded her bag and put it on the floor. "That was good, Mister. I still have enough for another good meal tonight." I started the car. Ella slurped the last of her Coke and then reached over and put her hand on my crotch, grabbing the zipper with practiced hands.

I pushed her hands away. "Put your seat belt on," I said.

She began to unbutton her blouse. "I'm woman enough for you."

"Button up, that's not why I bought you lunch."

In the quiet we reached Panik, and I stopped the car. "Here's my phone number." I gave her a business card. "Call me if you want to go to one of those nice places, I told you about."

"Listen," she said. "Gimme twenty dollars, would you, or he'll be angry. Please."

I gave her two tens and she opened the car door. "Don't forget your food," I said, and she took the bags and ran towards the building. I watched her holding them out as an offering, opening her arms wide to Panik as well as to her man. I drove off, my business card lying where Ella sat only minutes ago.

Dead Mother Shows Up at a Reunion

"You were a liar, cheat, thief, and con man," my brother said to me after he hugged me hello and steered us to the airport bar. He waved the waitress over and ordered a double gin and tonic. "Don't get me wrong, I love you and I've always loved you and looked up to you."
He looked at me as if to hear a response and when he didn't, he took a gulp to finish his drink and continued. "You never cared about anyone but yourself and I don't want to hear your crap about mommy beating you and telling you that you were an accident and not wanted. That has nothing to do with how you made her feel. She constantly cried over your behavior, and you can tell me all you want that if you didn't steal food from the market you worked at, we'd have gone hungry. Well let me tell you something, we would gladly have gone hungry than to have a thief in our midst bringing shame to mommy with every bite. She also knew where you were getting the money you brought home. You couldn't have earned that much at the corner market.
You keep writing stories about a mother who beats her son, who jabs at him with a broomstick while he hides under the bed, and don't you think that people know who you are writing about? Don't you care that making her life miserable when she was alive was enough so now you have to besmirch her memory while she's in her grave."

"You think this is funny? Waitress, bring me another. Right, a double. You caused nothing but grief. You committed fraud when you took pictures of the roller skaters at their convention and then couldn't deliver, and mommy had to make good on the money and she didn't have any money and you knew that. You know that story you tell about mixing up the chemicals when you developed the film is so much bull; it's so you. You were eleven and old enough to know better. You said you missed me and wanted to get together for a couple of days and catch up; well feel free to catch up. Maybe you don't want to talk about stealing her three silver dollars when you were eight, but she cried and cried when she found them gone.

And don't think I don't know you want to tell me that you paid for her grave and her funeral. You always made it clear that you blamed mommy because we grew up poor and you hated poor. Too bad. Live with it. You're almost sixty so get over it and never talk to me again about her.

Tell me. Why did you hate her so much that you made her cry every day? She never once, waitress another double please, she never once complained about you, but I'd see her crying and I'd ask her why and it was always you. You want another, No? Better that way; you could never hold your liquor. Why did you always have to get in trouble at school and make mommy go to the principal's office? Didn't you care? You stayed out late and never called and came home scuffed up like you were in fights all the time, but you always had a bankroll. So, what if you're the one who gave me my allowance all those years and bought me my first car. Where did the money come from? It wasn't honest money. Mom knew that and it broke her heart to take food and rent money from you.

One more and we'll leave the airport and go to our hotel and change and see the town and catch up. I hope you got us a decent hotel and a decent car. You did remember to rent a car, didn't you? It would be just like you to forget something as important as that. We can start getting reacquainted on the way to the hotel. I hope it's on the beach. Is it a good one with its own beach and pool? Does the pool have a swim up bar? You can afford those things. You only cared about making a lot of money and not how we felt at home so spend it, Mr. Big Shot. I can pay my share. I'm no free loader but you set up this get-together so you pay and by the way flying here economy sucked; I'll bet you didn't. Waitress . . .

Hey! Where are you going with your bag? The car rental's this way. You're heading towards the ticket agent. You never were very bright. I see nothing has changed."

Birthday Puppy

I didn't recognize the man who was standing in front of me when I opened the door, battered fedora in hand a mutt puppy in the crook of his arm.

He spoke in an unfamiliar voice. "I was once a good father, and you can repay me by giving me a place to stay. Here's the puppy I promised you for your tenth birthday."

I took the puppy, let him lick my face as this stranger unwrapped a cigar and stuck it in the corner of his mouth without bothering to light it. I noticed a large well-worn leather suitcase and as he reached down for it I shut the door on him.

He opened the unlocked door and muscled his suitcase inside. "At least thank me for the puppy or give it back," he said. "How about a drink or do you want to show me my room first?" he asked and sat on the couch,

I held the puppy and didn't look at him.

"The same old silent treatment your mother used on me. She taught you well." He handed me a wrinkled envelope from his inner pocket. "Your mother sent me this letter years ago; I want you to read it."

Ben, I'm sorry I kicked you out of the house. You were right. I shouldn't have spanked and yelled at Reuven so many times. I treated him like my mother treated me. That's all I knew about being a parent.

"How about that drink?" he asked.

I poured us each two fingers of bourbon, neat. I handed him his drink and he held it out to clink. I ignored the clink and drank mine down. I punched in Uber on my cell and carried his suitcase out to the front steps, then took his glass, still with his unfinished drink, and handed him the puppy and hustled him out of the house.

He started to say something, and I put up my hand and said, "You are not my father, I am not your son."

After I heard a car pull up in front of my house, I pushed the drape aside and watched him get into the car and drive off. I went out to have a smoke and as I sat on the steps the mutt puppy came over and sat next to me.

My Aunt Edith Accused Me of Being an Accomplice

My father's sister, my Aunt Edith called me at my Air Force
Base and said her brother, Uncle Lou, was dead and I should
send her $1000 to pay for half his burial expense since he
jumped out of his hotel window a couple of weeks after we
met for the first time and she knows I must've said
something to cause it, but I thought back to my visit with
Uncle Lou but I never told my aunt what happened or sent
her any money. And I tossed her letters without opening
them.

Paul Beckman

Badges of Mourning

After dressing, Sarah cut a piece of cloth from her mother's apron pocket, a corner of her father's tallit with the fringes, and a piece of her brother's baseball uniform sleeve with his number and safety-pinned them in a row above her left breast. Then, leaving the hotel, she took a cab to the synagogue.

Inside, she walked down the aisle approaching the coffins and spotted the Rabbi. She walked over. She told him she was Sarah and took her coat off. Please rip these mourning ribbons and say the blessing she said pointing at her handiwork. He asked the meaning of each. She told him. They were outside the doorway of the ante room holding the mourning family leaving room for well-wishers. The Rabbi reached into his pocket and took out a black ribbon but Sarah insisted on three black ribbons with safety pins and one by one pinned a black ribbon and said a prayer after cutting the ribbons up the middle with scissors. He said the English and Hebrew names of her sons and her husband who lay in the coffins, but he did not touch the safety-pinned pieces from her parents and brother who sat in the mourners' room looking at her. They hadn't seen each other in the five years she'd walked out on her family to be with another.

The Rabbi motioned for her to go into the mourners' room to be with the family before starting the service, but she turned and walked to the caskets and stood dry-eyed and motionless, head bowed, hands-on each coffin until she was gently prodded away so the funeral service could begin.

Speaking Evil

"Don't speak evil of the dead," my dead Mother said.
"Since when is telling the truth speaking evil?" I asked her.
"Listen, don't play games with me. There is a difference, and
you know it."
"Give me an example of my speaking evil of the dead. Who?"
"Me. Your Mother. That's who."
"There you go again, Mom. I never spoke against you."
"Last night," she interrupted. "You did it again last night."
"You mean my telling the story of hiding from you under the
bed? And you jabbing at me with a broomstick so I would get
out from under the bed so you could give me a real beating?"
"Yes. That story."
"Well. Did I lie?"
"It's how you tell the story."
"Did I lie or embellish the story?"
"You didn't lie, but you made me sound evil."
"I was eight years old. You were jabbing an eight-year-old
boy with a broomstick as hard as you could because I was
hiding under the bed. You could've poked my eye out."
"I would never poke your eye out. You shouldn't have
knocked over the gumball machine and broke it—sending
gumballs everywhere."
"What could an eight-year-old boy do that was so bad to get
treated like that? Make me understand and I'll never tell the
story again."
"How can you say I'd poke your eye out? What kind of
mother will people take me for? The dead have enough
problems."
"Mom, tell me. Is it OK for the dead to speak evil against the
dead?"
"Go. I won't bother you anymore. Tell everyone. Say
anything you want."
"I never tell anyone about the iron, Mom. Doesn't that
count?"

Paul Beckman

New York State of Mind

A friend and I took a train from Connecticut to New York. I
spotted my only rich relatives near Rockefeller Center and
crossed the street to say hello. My great uncle, great aunt and
their bratty kid all said they didn't know who I was. I
mentioned my mother's name as well as my grandfathers who
was my aunt's brother and others in the family and they knew
them but hustled my ragamuffin ass away. I told my mother
when I got home and she said I was making it up but I was so
insistent she called and they said no, I never approached
them, but they were at Rockefeller center that day and time.
To this day I don't know if I approached them or not.

Dear Mom

Dear Mom . . . You were sure right about the foliage. The Green is ablaze with multi-colored trees and the constant changing hues made me want to draw or paint them so I bought a small colored pencil kit and have included a couple of sketches. Hope they're not too abstract for your liking. I'm also taking photos of the trees and have purposely blurred them so shapes don't interfere with the colors. It's starting to get chilly here now so I'm glad you had me pack those sweaters. I guess autumn (you always call it fall) is the best season on both coasts. Too bad I won't be seeing you for Thanksgiving, I was looking forward to it; but if you say you're physically and mentally exhausted and need the rest who am I to argue? Love Reuven

Dear Mom . . . I don't know what to say except that I'm sorry about you and Marty. I've known for a long time the marriage wasn't perfect but I had no idea he would just up and leave you as dad did. Are you sure you don't want me to come home for the semester break? It's five weeks and I can get a lot done around the house for you. I was looking forward to sharing my experiences with you, seeing the old crowd, and sleeping in my old bed. I do miss that old bed! I understand that I remind you of Dad but I'm not him and I hope you'll reconsider. Your loving son Reuven.

Dear Mom . . . You forgot to send me your new phone number when you had it changed and went unlisted. I tried to call you on your birthday. Did you do anything special? The break's been over for a couple of weeks and the new courses are like the weather—tough. I'm not used to this much snow and we've been getting plenty of it. The other day I got thinking about your cooking and I desperately wanted your chicken fricassee. I couldn't get it out of my mind, so I went down to a Greek diner and ordered it at one in the morning. You could sure give them cooking lessons. Their attempt at fricassee only made me more homesick. I can't wait to come home for the summer. I've been in touch with Burt and he's promised to hire me back at the Columbia Market. Love, Reuven

Dear Mom . . . It's too bad you don't have real recipes, just some notes that you improvise from. If you should happen to think about it when you're cooking one of your old standards please write down the ingredients and instructions as you cook. I'd really appreciate it. The salmon croquets I had at the diner last week were nothing like yours, and the same with the meatloaf and stew. P.S. phone number? Love

Dear Lily . . .It sure does feel strange calling you anything but Mom, but if that makes you feel better, I'm glad to do it. Are you going to be here for my graduation? It's been years since we've seen each other and I want you to meet my girlfriend and be with me on my big day. I wish you hadn't returned the yearbook photo of me. I can't help it if you see "him" every time you look at me. Reuven

Dear Lily . . . You missed a great wedding, and it would have been much greater if you'd have been here. Sara and her parents had been hoping to meet you. We were expecting to see you on our honeymoon trip and dropped by the house to surprise you. I had no idea you moved. At least you kept your old PO Box. I started my new job the week we got back. It's a wonderful career opportunity as assistant to the comptroller of the phone company. Reuven

Lily . . . Sorry to upset you. I had no idea he once worked for the phone company. R

Dear Lily . . . Haven't heard back from my recent letters. Hope all is okay. The baby's six months old now and Sara's a great mother —like you were. I'd love to send you a picture of Sammy but I have to tell you that he looks exactly like I did at his age.

Dear Mom . . . Don't worry, I won't send the photo. It is nice having my old grade school stuff and photo albums but it's also kind of sad. The boxes arrived last week. I can't help it that my handwriting is the same as "his" so I'm writing this on my computer. Hope it's easier for you to handle. Sammy's starting kindergarten and Emma's in nursery school. Sara decided to go back to school for her master's and I have just been promoted to Comptroller. Reuven

Mom . . . It's my way of wording things as much as the handwriting, you say. Some things can't be helped. Love Reuven

Lily . . . I can't tell you how disappointed I have been to not hear from you this past year. If I don't get a response to this letter, I'll stop writing. Meanwhile, I hope that all is well with you. I never mentioned that Marty looked me up when I was at college and visited often. He was at my graduation, wedding and around for the babies when they needed a grandparent—which has been all of their lives. I know that he was a good man and didn't walk out on you—you threw him out. That was probably one of the best days of his life. I called him Dad because he treated me like his son. He's been living in an apartment a few blocks away from us. Last week he died. R

Lily. . . What am I supposed to do with your phone number now? R

Hey Residents!

On my monthly train ride from New Haven to New York I
always look at the projects in Bridgeport where I grew up.
Last month I saw a half dozen of the apartments' windows
and doors were boarded over and each subsequent week
there were more and more until yesterday Marina Village was
a ghost town of asphalt and brick with large bulldozers, a
wrecking ball on a crane and a row of dump trucks lined up,
sentinel-like, to take my childhood away.
I picked up my car in New Haven and drove back to
Bridgeport and parked in a tight space in the parking lot,
something I wouldn't have done before, and walked through
the asphalt jungle as John Huston so aptly named his movie.
It was dusk, the fog covering thick and low as I passed a
couple of buildings heading towards my old one. I saw a blur
of orange and walked closer and there was a group of twenty
or so men in orange jumpsuits with "RESIDENT" stenciled
across their backs. They were black, Puerto Rican and white.
Some were exercising, some playing cards, a few talking in
small groups, and most were smoking. I knew them all and I
walked closer, and they turned and stood as a barrier to keep
me from entering their area.
Hey, Joey, Leroy, Juan, Mickey, I called. No one answered
and saw their faces were young faces on old bodies and when
the light struck a different way their faces became old—older
and harder looking than our age should have fostered. They
resumed their game-playing ritual without responding to me
and I walked around the building towards my old apartment.
I heard the train go by and the din of the cars on the adjacent
interstate and I wondered how I lived there with all the noise.
I stopped to watch a group of teens in the corner of the
parking lot shooting craps against the curb. I knew them all
and one was me, looking back at me, as he blew on the dice
and rolled and then picked up the bills in the center and
rolled again.

I moved on and had no problem finding my apartment, my mother sitting on the stoop with the next-door neighbor drinking coffee, their wash in baskets ready to hang on the line. The bricks in the building moved in ripples. My bedroom window was not boarded nor was the door. In order to get in, I'd have to walk around my mother, or our neighbor would have to move aside but neither did. I saw my brother looking out the bedroom window at me and I waved but he didn't respond.

I headed back to my car and there were all the people from the Village out and about and I felt as if I were walking a gauntlet getting back to my car which had a couple of the guys from my youth sitting on the hood. They moved towards me, their faces no more the young faces but drinkers faces with veined red noses, rheumy eyes, and their walk a jailhouse shuffle.

I drove home to my comfortable life in the New Haven burbs. In the morning I went out to the garage to get my car and saw that it had graffiti all over it, but we didn't call it graffiti back then. Jew boy, faggot, loser, creep, punk, and other reminders written in crayon and chalk that I hadn't noticed last night when I walked to my car. The following week, I saw from the train, the wrecking crew had done their job and only the dozers remained. It seemed like such a small piece of property to hold so many people and memories.

ABOUT THE AUTHOR

Paul Beckman's last flash collection, "Kiss Kiss" was a finalist for the Best Indie Awards for short story collections 2019. Paul had a micro-story selected for the 2018 Norton Anthology New Micro Exceptionally Short Fiction, was one of the winners in the 2016 *The Best Small Fictions* and his story "Mom's Goodbye" was chosen as the winner of the 2016 Fiction Southeast Editor's Prize. Paul was nominated for the 2019 Best Small fiction series and had a story accepted for the 2022 Best of Microfictions. He's widely published with over 750 stories. Paul hosts the monthly Zoom FBomb global flash fiction reading series.

Printed in the USA
CPSIA information can be obtained
at www.ICGtesting.com
JSHW082049171023
50142JS00002B/66